There was great excitement in the forest. The sound of voices wakened Friend Owl. He leaned over and saw a newborn fawn huddled against his mother, surrounded by a crowd of animals.

Since early morning, Thumper the rabbit had been spreading the good news. "Wake up! The little prince is born!" The forest animals had come from near and far to admire him.

In the company of his new friends, little Bambi
set out to explore the clearing, the forest and
the world. Thumper was proud to teach him
what he knew.

"There are lots of different plants and animals
in the forest." But something special had
caught the fawn's eye. "Oh, that's a butterfly,"
Thumper explained.

"But-but-butterfly!" Bambi repeated.

Bambi was very happy in the forest.
He made friends, and his mother
taught him all sorts of things:
what plants could be eaten, where
water would always be found, and
all about Man.

The little fawn listened carefully,
and asked all sorts of questions.
But then he was ready to play.
Not far away he saw something
very interesting.

It was a pool! Bambi leaned over, then backed away in confusion. Another fawn was doing exactly what he did!

"It's only your reflection," his mother explained. "But can you tell me what that is?"

Nearby, Bambi saw another reflection. He hid behind his mother. "You're not afraid, are you?" his mother asked. "Here is a friend for you. Her name is Faline."

Bambi was very happy to have Faline as a friend. But one day, right in the middle of their play, the whole forest started rushing past. Bambi and Faline were knocked about as rabbits scampered between their legs.

A herd of stags darted by. Then Bambi's mother rushed over, crying, "Quick, Bambi! Follow us. Man is in the forest!"

The deer hid in the deepest part of the forest. "When there is danger, you must come and hide here," explained his mother.

"The hunters won't come this way?" Bambi asked.

"No, it's too far for them. And more importantly, it's your father's territory. He will protect you."

Just then a magnificent stag appeared from the shadows. "I am your father, Bambi, the Great Prince of the Forest. One day, when you are grown, you will take my place."

Bambi was too impressed to speak.

One morning a few days later, the cold awakened Bambi. When he looked out, he saw a thick white blanket covering the ground. The little fawn was so surprised that he stood for a moment without moving. "It's beautiful!" he cried.

He set out running to warm himself up — and fell down.

"Bambi, there's a trick to sliding on ice. You should have waited for me to show you," said Thumper, laughing.
Then he helped Bambi get up.

Snow continued to fall. It covered everything, and soon it became difficult to find plants to eat. "I'm awful hungry, Mother," Bambi said.

His mother taught him how to gnaw the bark off trees and dig up roots. "Be patient," she said. "Spring will come again."

Suddenly, gunfire rang out. "Run, Bambi! Run and hide! Don't look back!" his mother said.

Bambi ran deep into the forest. Terrified and out of breath, he finally stopped, looked back and called his mother. But she wasn't there behind him. He was alone! Bambi began to cry. "Mother, where are you?"

Suddenly Bambi's father appeared beside him. "Your mother can't be with you any more. Man has taken her away. Now you must be brave. Come, my son."

The days passed, and Bambi began to forget his sadness. By the time spring came again, he had grown into a magnificent young stag.

One morning, he ran into his friend, Thumper. He had grown up too, and had a pretty female rabbit with him. Flower the skunk had also found a new friend.

Bambi wanted to play, but his friends were too busy. Then one day Bambi heard a familiar voice. "What's the matter, Bambi? Don't you remember me?"

It was Faline. Bambi was shy because she had become so beautiful.

But Faline encouraged him. "Come and walk with me," she said.

Suddenly, a fierce young stag named Ronno
burst out of the woods. "She's coming with me!
Get out of here!" he ordered.

Bambi realized that if he wanted to be with
Faline, he would have to fight. The two young
stags hurled themselves at each other, and
their antlers clashed. Finally, Bambi drove
Ronno away.

Bambi and Faline looked tenderly at each
other, knowing that nothing could separate
them now.

Many days later, Bambi and his father noticed a strange odor in the air. Some hunters had forgotten to put out their fire!

The fire spread rapidly, and the forest began to burn. The animals raced to escape the flames and reach safety. It was hard to breathe because of the smoke.

Bambi ran to find Faline, but he didn't see her anywhere. He ran until he fell to the ground, exhausted.

"You must get up, Bambi," his father said.

Bambi pulled himself up and followed his father.

At last they reached the river, but they still had to cross it. On the opposite bank the other animals watched the approaching fire. What a relief it was when Bambi and his father joined them, safe and sound.

Best of all, Faline was there! "Bambi, you're safe!" she cried. "I was so afraid."

After the great forest fire, Bambi's father decided that it was time for Bambi to become the new Prince of the Forest.

So Bambi took his father's place. He proved worthy of the task that had been passed onto him, and protected those around him.

He and Faline were very happy together. And the following spring, Faline brought not only one, but two lovely fawns into the world.

The faithful Thumper announced the news:
Bambi was a father! All the animals of the
forest gathered to admire the newborn fawns.

Meanwhile, Bambi climbed to a rocky height
above the trees and looked over his domain.
His father would be very proud.